This is Ballerina Becky. She is a
very graceful ballerina, and she
hardly ever wobbles.

A catalogue record for this book is available from the British Library

Published by Ladybird Books Ltd
80 Strand London WC2R 0RL
A Penguin Company

2 4 6 8 10 9 7 5 3 1

© LADYBIRD BOOKS LTD MMIV

Illustrations © Emma Dodd MMIV

LADYBIRD and the device of a Ladybird are trademarks of Ladybird Books Ltd

Little Workmates

Ballerina Becky

by Mandy Ross
illustrated by Emma Dodd

Ladybird

"It's the Story Town Ballet tonight!" said Ballerina Becky, setting off early to Doctor Daisy's for a checkup on her sore knee.

"Gosh, it's windy," she said, wobbling a little on her way.

Doctor Daisy unwrapped the bandage on Ballerina Becky's leg.

"Your knee has healed beautifully," she said.

"Just in time for the ballet," said Becky. "Are you going to come?"

"Try to stop me," said Doctor Daisy. "I'm sure all of Story Town will be there."

"But what if I feel nervous and start wobbling?" asked Ballerina Becky.

"Just close your eyes and imagine yourself dancing beautifully," said Doctor Daisy. "Then you'll be fine!"

Ballerina Becky practised her leaps and arabesques all the way home. When she got back, Postman Pete was ringing her doorbell.

"Parcel for you, Becky," he said. "Phew, it's windy this morning, isn't it!"

Ballerina Becky opened
the parcel.

"My fairy tutu and wings!
Just in time for the ballet,"
she said.

Just then, PC Polly
walked past.

"Look at my costume!"
called Becky.

"You'll look lovely!"
smiled PC Polly.

But then...oh, no! A gust of
wind tugged the fairy wings
right out of Becky's hands.

Up and up they flew. At last
they stopped, tangled high
in the branches of a tree.

"How can I dance without my fairy wings?" cried Ballerina Becky.

But PC Polly was thinking hard.

"Don't worry," she said, getting out her walkie-talkie. "Hello, yes, it's an emergency."

Soon – Nee-naw! Nee-naw!
It was Fireman Fergus in
his fire engine.

Fergus got out his
longest ladder and
climbed up the tree.
Carefully, he
untangled Becky's
wings from
the branches.

"Oh, PC Polly and Fireman Fergus, thank you!" gasped Ballerina Becky. "You are coming to the Story Town Ballet tonight, aren't you?"

"My shift finishes just in time," nodded Fireman Fergus.

At last, it was time for the ballet. Ballerina Becky put on her fairy tutu and wings. She looked like a real fairy princess, but inside she felt a bit wobbly.

Then she remembered what Doctor Daisy had said. She closed her eyes and imagined herself dancing beautifully.

Ballerina Becky was the star of the Story Town Ballet. She danced like a true fairy princess, flittering and fluttering across the stage without even a single wobble!

"Hurray for Ballerina Becky," cried all of Story Town. "The best fairy princess ever!"

Footballer Fabio

Vet Vicky

Doctor Daisy

Builder Bill

Postman Pete

Fireman Fergus

Nurse Nancy